Freddie Saves the Day

Jon Acevski and David Ashton

WARNER BOOKS

Freddie Saves the Day
A Warner Book

First published in Great Britain in 1992 by Warner Books

Copyright © Hollywood Road Film Productions Limited 1992

The moral right of the authors has been asserted.

Design by Between The Lines
Illustrated by HRFP Artists
Adaptation by Belinda Hollyer

All rights reserved.

A CIP catalogue record for this book is available from the British Library.

ISBN 0 356 20116 3

Printed by Graphicom SRL, Italy

Warner Books
A Division of Little, Brown and Company (UK) Limited
165 Great Dover Street
London SE1 4YA

The Freddie Library

Have you read all the Freddie books? These are the titles:

FREDDIE AS FR07
PRINCE FREDERIC   THE ISLE OF WORMS
FREDDIE GOES TO LONDON   FREDDIE SAVES THE DAY

All Freddie books are available at your bookshop or newsagent, or can be ordered from:
Little, Brown and Company (UK) Limited, PO Box 11, Falmouth, Cornwall TR10 9EN.
Alternately you may fax your order to the above address on: 0326 376423.

Payments can be made as follows: cheque, postal order (payable to Little, Brown and Company)
or credit card, Visa/Access, with card number and expiry date. Do not send cash or currency.
UK customers and BFPO allow £1.00 for postage and packing for the first book, plus 50p for the
second book, plus 30p for each additional book up to a maximum charge of £3.00 (7 books plus).
Overseas customers including Ireland allow £2.00 for the first book
plus £1.00 for the second book plus 50p for each additional book.

El Supremo's Maximum Ray box had begun to work. The strange red light, filled with all the energies from the stolen buildings, now turned into an evil force.

And the rays had penetrated everywhere in Britain, sending the whole country to sleep.

At El Supremo's headquarters deep beneath the Isle of Worms, Daffers was helpless in enemy hands, indoctrinated in the Power of the Snake.

Scotty, exhausted and shivering, waited on a rock in the North Sea, while Freddie and Nessie sped off to get help, before it was too late.

But El Supremo had already given his submarine commander the order to attack Britain, while everyone was asleep.

"Thank you, El Supremo," grated the submarine commander. Then he turned to his crews.

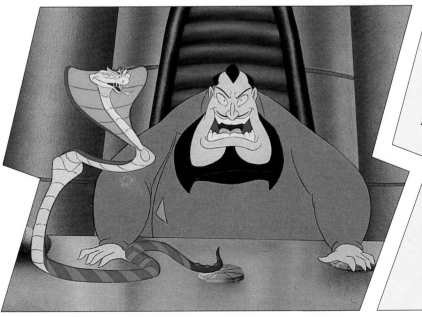

"Full speed ahead!" he ordered.
Was everything lost? And where - oh where - was Freddie?

Many miles away, Freddie and
Nessie arrived at Nessie's cave,
an underwater world of
extraordinary grace and beauty.

Freddie was so amazed by
everything, he almost forgot
why they had come!

He was surprised to see other animals like Nessie there, too. "I thought there was only one of you, my dear Nessie!"

"Not at all," replied Nessie with a smile. "This is my family!"

"Granny," asked a very small Nessie, "is that Freddie the Frog, from the story you're always telling us? Freddie with magical powers, who moved the rock and saved your tail?"

And Nessie nodded, laughing.

There was so much to look at, and so many of Nessie's friends and relations to meet, that Freddie felt quite overwhelmed.
Everyone wanted to be introduced to the famous Freddie whom Nessie had talked about so often.

Only when all the introductions were over, could Freddie and Nessie get down to business.

8

"Now, what was it you were wanting, Freddie?" asked Nessie.

"A little help from my friends!" replied Freddie.

And as soon as Freddie had explained what he needed, a whole army of Nessie's relations headed off for the Isle of Worms and the enemy submarines.

When they arrived, they quickly tied strong seaweed ropes around the propellers of the submarines. They were only just in time to stop them launching their attack!

On board his submarine, the Commander was in a rage. Why were the submarines not moving?

"What's the matter, you imbeciles?" he shouted. "I said full steam ahead!"

But the submarines were locked together, in a helpless circle.

"Thank you Nessie - see you later!" called Freddie . . .

. . . and he shot off through the dark North Sea waters, towards the Isle of Worms.

Scotty was still sat shivering on the rock when Freddie burst from the water near him.

Freddie leaped on to the rock. "Now we'll go and get Daffers!" he announced, as he pulled Scotty to his feet, and set off for a secret underwater entrance he had noticed earlier.

But how could they get past the guards?

Freddie's plan was simple. First, he jumped into Scotty's arms, and pretended to be unconscious. Then Scotty followed his instructions and staggered towards the guards.

"Help, help!" called Scotty. "I've just come across a large dead frog!"

When the guards rushed forward to look, Freddie kicked out with both his powerful legs, and caught the two guards under their chins. They were knocked out! Then Freddie and Scotty put on their uniforms, and walked calmly inside El Supremo's headquarters.

Deep inside, Daffers was
being taken down a corridor
by some guards, when she
saw two other guards coming
towards them.

One of them was wearing
large, flipper-like shoes -
and Daffers recognised
them at once. It was
Freddie, in disguise!

Daffers checked to see if the guards had noticed anything, but they hadn't. Then, just as Freddie and Scotty had passed, Freddie suddenly turned back. He grabbed the guards by their necks and gave a quick squeeze - and they tumbled unconscious to the ground.

"Oh Freddie," laughed Daffers in relief. "Give me frogs any day. I've gone right off snakes!"

The three companions headed for the treasure chamber, with Freddie and Scotty pretending to be Daffers's guards.

"What's the password?" asked the treasure chamber guard, suspecting nothing.

"*Freddie* shall rule the world!" cried Daffers, as Freddie suddenly knocked out the guard. Then they dashed into the treasure chamber, and locked the door behind them.

Inside the heroes confronted a gang of guards, masked to protect themselves against the Maximum Ray which still poured from the glassy box.

The guards stood, surprised and confused, as Freddie and Scotty took off their guards' uniforms, and before they could move, threw them into their faces.

The fight had begun!

With Daffers putting her tai chi to good use . . .

20

. . . and Scotty wielding his haggis-shaped baton . . .

. . . and Freddie leaping and kicking, the guards were quickly overcome. But just as the last guard fell to the ground . . .

. . . he knocked against the glassy box. It swung around, and the Maximum Ray was directed straight at Daffers and Scotty!

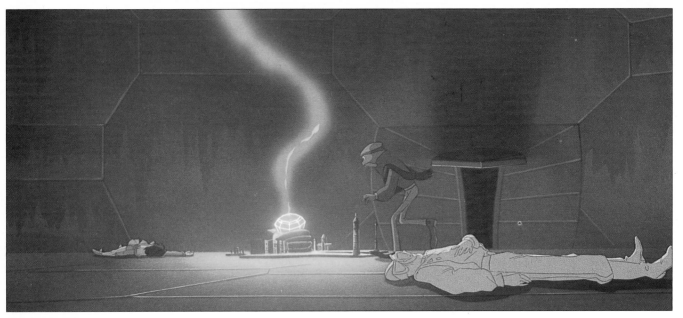

They collapsed to the floor, leaving Freddie to summon up all his magical strength as he struggled against the Maximum Ray. He finally managed to heave the box up and throw it across the room.

The box exploded - and the evil rays were no more!

But Freddie, too, had fallen to the ground unconscious. And just then, an alarm sounded in the control room.

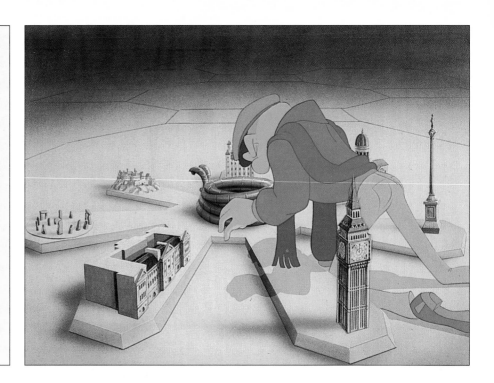

24

"The Ray!" gasped El Supremo. "The Maximum Ray has stopped!"

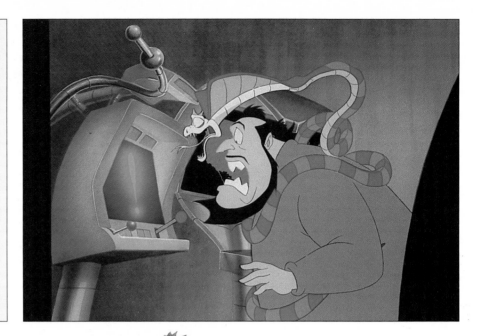

"FR07 must have penetrated our defences and reached the treasure chamber!"

Panic-stricken, El Supremo and Messina rushed to the treasure chamber.

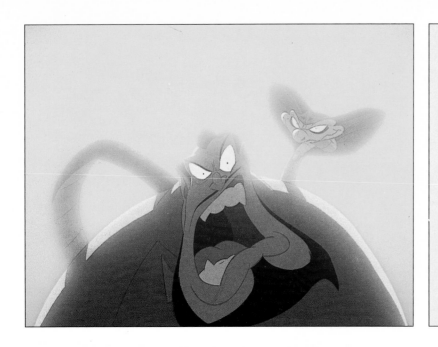

"I will kill him!" spat El Supremo, in rage and fear. And there, on the floor, lay Freddie, Daffers and Scotty, all three of them still unconscious.

El Supremo raised his arms in triumph! Freddie and his companions were helpless.

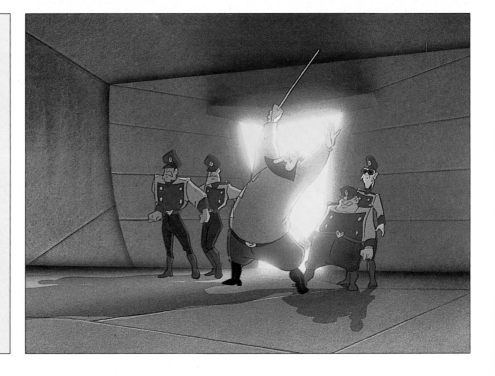

In the meantime, people all over Britain were waking up again, as the effects of the Maximum Ray wore off.
In the Albert Hall, the conductor and orchestra sat up, and started playing again, where they had stopped.

The audience carried on singing along, as if nothing had happened.
"Britons never,
    never, never,
Shall be slaves!"

And in Wembley Stadium, the footballer finally scored his goal!

Daffers and Scotty, too, were beginning to recover. They got slowly to their feet. But Freddie still lay unconscious on the floor.

As everyone watched, El Supremo headed towards Freddie's body with death in his eyes. "You have tried to destroy my plan, FR07, but you have not succeeded!"

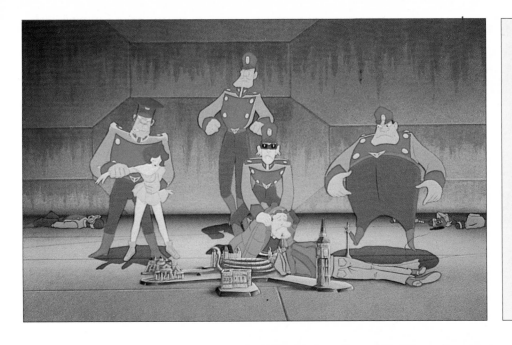

"My submarines have already landed - you are too late!" cried El Supremo, not realising that his subs had been tied up by Nessie and her family.

El Supremo raised his laser sword. "And now, FRO7, you die!"

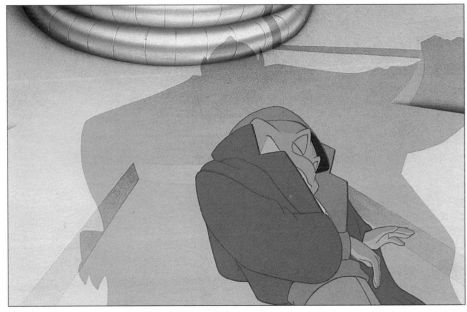

But as Freddie lay there, unable to move, his mind flashed back . . .

. . . back to his
childhood, as
a boy prince.

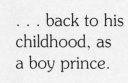

"Fear not the
sword," said his
father, the
Magician King.
"The true
powers of the
mind are
greater than
any weapon . . ."

And just as Daffers cried out in fear to Freddie . . .

. . . Freddie's amazing powers returned to him! He stopped the sword in mid-air, and threw El Supremo across the room, like a toy! Even the guards' guns were no match for Freddie's powers . . .

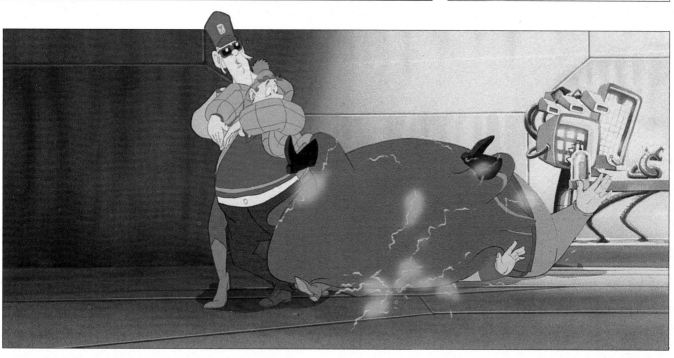

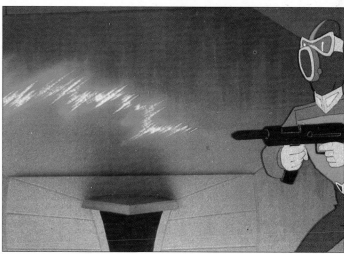

. . . as he turned
them into butterflies!

But Daffers had no choice but to use less peaceful tactics against her opponents.

And as the bullets started to fly at Scotty, Daffers told him to activate his barrel shield. The bullets stuck harmlessly to its surface – Scotty was safe!

In no time, all the guards had been disposed of, and only El Supremo was left standing. Freddie turned his back in contempt, and rejoined his companions.

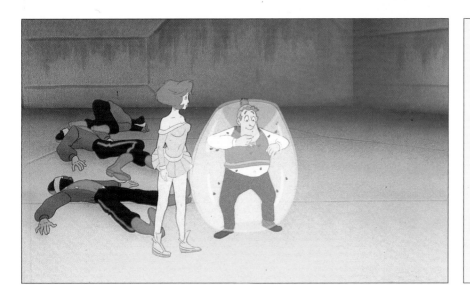

"So," said Freddie, "the job is over now. Take off your barrel shield, Scotty."

And the three companions walked away, ignoring their defeated enemy.

But El Supremo couldn't bear that! He hit out wildly with his laser sword, and then rushed towards them, his sword raised to strike.

But just as he did so . . .

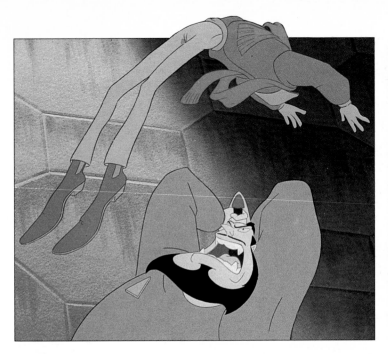

. . . Freddie's agility won once more. "It seems as if you have lost your strike," he mocked.

But El Supremo had another idea. Lunging upwards, he rushed across the room and lifted the sword over Big Ben with an evil light in his eyes.

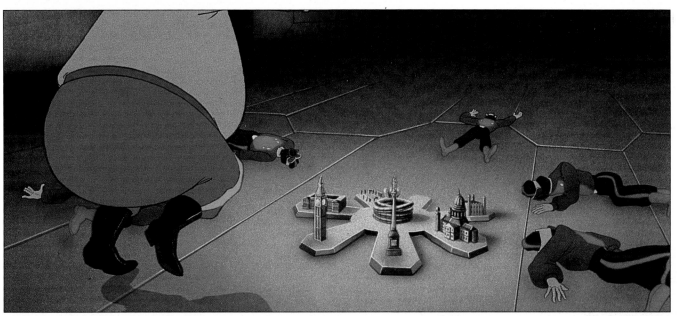

"Surrender, FRO7, or I will destroy your precious monument!"

Freddie immediately raised his arms. "Please don't destroy it - the Queen of England would never forgive me. I surrender - I'm prepared to die for it!" And Freddie moved slowly towards El Supremo.

"No, Freddie!" cried Daffers.

"It seems I have no choice," replied Freddie but he still managed to signal with his eyes to Daffers.

Quickly, Daffers saw what Freddie meant - the miniaturising machine, on the desk!

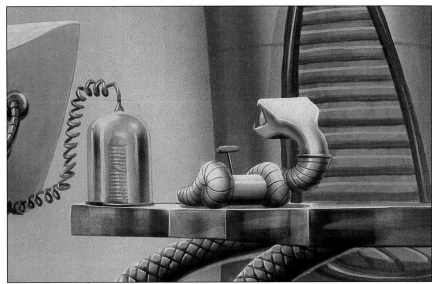

El Supremo didn't notice when Daffers moved towards the desk. "The time has come, FRO7, for your departure!" And El Supremo laughed wildly as he raised his sword over Freddie.

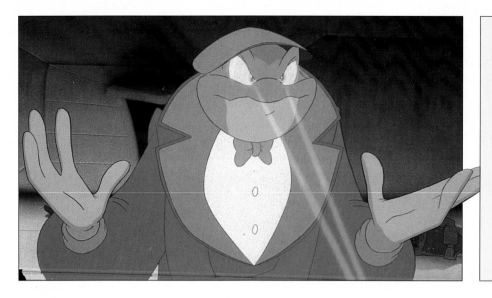

But as Freddie was concentrating all his powers on Big Ben, to move it under El Supremo, Daffers was pointing the miniaturising machine towards it.

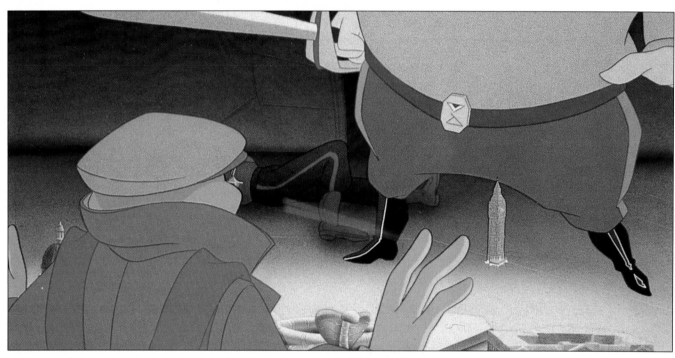

Freddie signalled, and Daffers pulled the lever. But Big Ben grew even smaller!

42

"Keep your hands up," growled El Supremo to Freddie.

"Ah yes - up! Up!" said Freddie signalling to Daffers at the same time.

So Daffers pushed the lever up -

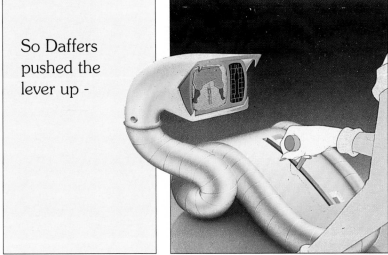

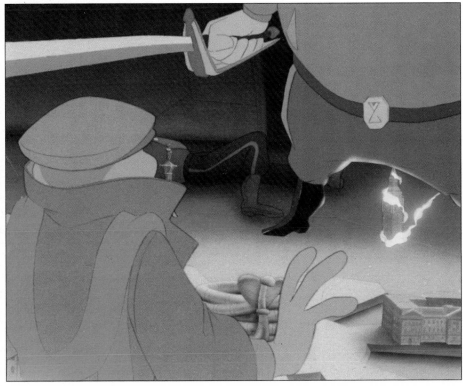

– and Big Ben suddenly grew, shooting to the ceiling –

– and taking El Supremo with it on the clock hands!

"As you said - the *time* has come!" laughed Freddie.

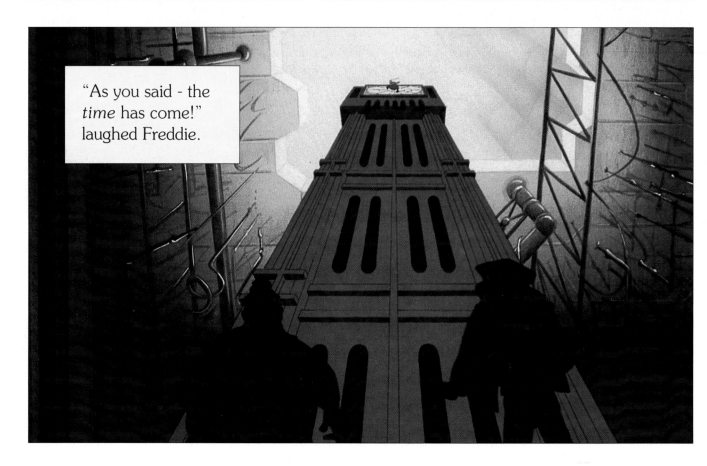

And then the companions adjusted the control, until Big Ben was back to its miniature size again, with a tiny El Supremo dangling on the clock face.

Back in London, the Brigadier had woken up. "Oh dear, I thought Big Ben had come back home. I saw it, I swear." He looked around sadly. "It must have been a dream."

The Brigadier's telephone rang - it was Daffers, from the Isle of Worms. "That's right, Brigadier," said Daffers. "We've got all the missing monuments, and we've won the battle!"

"It's perfectly safe," she continued. "The enemy is totally destroyed . . ."

But Daffers had forgotten about Messina the Snake!

"Destroyed?" hissed Messina. "Not as far as I'm concerned. You may think you have won, but I intend to change all that . . ."

And only Freddie's quick thinking saved Daffers.

"Stay out of this," Freddie warned Daffers and Scotty. "This is a family affair."

"Why don't you reveal yourself in your true colours, my dear Aunt Messina?"

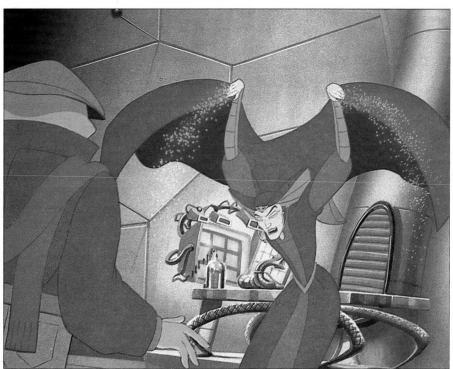

"So, Frederic," replied Messina, "we meet again! This time you will not escape!"

"I'm not the little frog I was so long ago," said Freddie. "I do not fear you now. Whatever ugly shape you take, I shall defeat you!"

But how would he stand up to his old enemy now, for she turned into a vampire bat and flew straight for Freddie's throat.

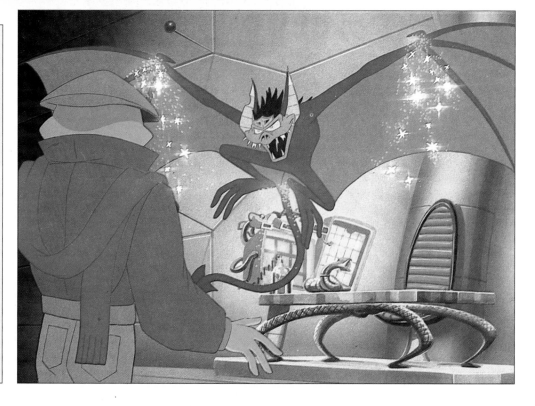

48

Freddie jumped aside, and the bat crashed into the wall. But all was not over, for Messina then turned into a dangerous hyena.

The hyena charged, Freddie jumped in the air – and it crashed into the desk.

Then there was a
sinister silence.
"Look out behind
you, Freddie!" called
Daffers suddenly.

"On the floor!" yelled Scotty.
   Freddie looked down just in time to move
away from the scorpion. "Three
against one isn't fair,"
complained the
scorpion.

So Freddie danced nimbly around with the scorpion, until she was exhausted.

"You're getting too old for this," laughed Freddie. But just as he put a large glass bowl over the scorpion to trap her . . .

. . . she changed into a giant python, and burst through the bowl. As quick as a flash, the python wrapped herself around the helpless Freddie.

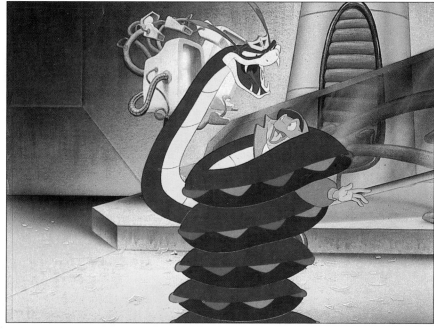

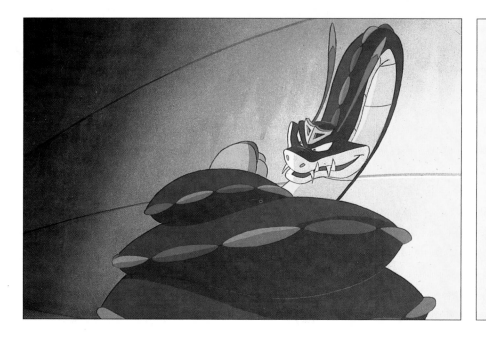

"Are you running out of breath, dear nephew?" asked Messina, as she gave him another deadly hug.

As Freddie's eyes glazed over, he suddenly remembered something his father, the Magician King, had once told him.

Outside the castle, Frederic had run into his father's arms.

"Ooh," he gasped, "I'm all out of breath."

"Your strength will always be *beyond* your last breath," replied his father.

Spurred on, Freddie suddenly snapped open his eyes.

He drew on his final store of energy, and strained and stretched against the coils of the python. Suddenly they loosened, and Freddie grabbed hold of Messina's head and swung her round and round, faster and faster.

Then finally, he released her!

The python crashed into the ceiling and wrapped herself around the girder. Messina was badly hurt.

Slowly and painfully, the python turned into a vulture, with a broken wing. "One day you will pay for this!" croaked Messina, as she flapped awkwardly away.

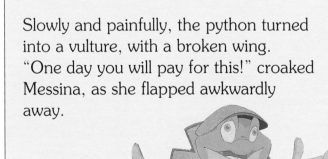

Just then, the Brigadier arrived.

"My goodness! What kind of creature was that?" he asked.
    "No one of importance," replied Freddie. "Just some ugly old bird!"

Taking the Brigadier into the treasure chamber, the three companions showed him the miniature buildings. A tiny El Supremo still hung from the hands of Big Ben.

Freddie put El Supremo into a matchbox, and presented him to the Brigadier.

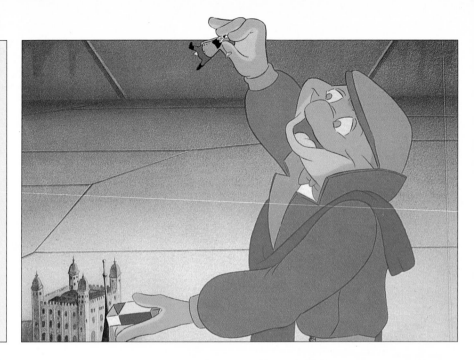

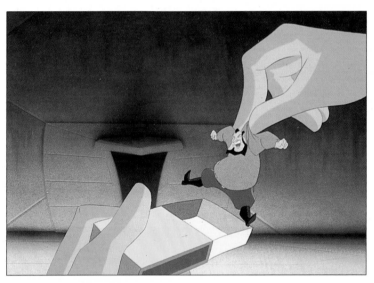

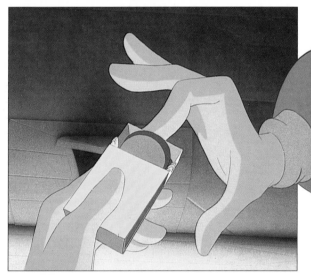

"Well," said Freddie, "it's time we went home. There is one more job to do!"

58

Back in London the Brigadier asked Freddie how he knew that Trilby was a spy for El Supremo.

Freddie laughed. "Because of the way he told the time!"

"Take this traitor away," ordered the Brigadier.

Huge crowds had gathered at Buckingham Palace, waiting for the building to be returned. Freddie handed the miniaturising machine to the Queen, and showed her how to use it.

"All you have to do is pull the lever, Your Majesty . . ."

The Queen was so pleased, she told the Brigadier to offer Freddie a knighthood.

"Thank you, Your Majesty, but I'm not sure my President would approve," replied Freddie, bowing low.

"And now," said the Brigadier, "a little celebration! Three cheers for Freddie!"

Then the phone rang – it was a call from the United States for the Brigadier.

"Of *course*, Mr President. If you *need* him, FRO7 - *plus* assistants - will be on the next Concorde flight to Washington!"

Then he turned to the room. "So, ladies and gentlemen, may I propose a toast: to America . . ."

"And to FRO7!" added Scotty.

Daffers beckoned Freddie to the window.

"Look, you seem to have another fan club, Freddie!" she laughed.

Freddie was delighted to see Nessie swimming along the Thames.

"Well," smiled Freddie,
"here's to our next
adventure!"